Acting Edition

I0591861

the bandaged place

by Harrison David Rivers

ISBN 978-0-573-71067-4

www.concordtheatricals.com
www.concordtheatricals.co.uk

FOR PRODUCTION INQUIRIES

UNITED STATES AND CANADA
info@concordtheatricals.com
1-866-979-0447

UNITED KINGDOM AND EUROPE
licensing@concordtheatricals.co.uk
020-7054-7298

Each title is subject to availability from Concord Theatricals Corp.,
depending upon country of performance. Please be aware that *the
bandaged place* may not be licensed by Concord Theatricals Corp. in
your territory. Professional and amateur producers should contact the
nearest Concord Theatricals Corp. office or licensing partner to verify
availability.

MUSIC AND THIRD-PARTY MATERIALS USE NOTE

IMPORTANT BILLING AND CREDIT REQUIREMENTS

the bandaged place was produced by Roundabout Theatre Company (Todd Haimes, Artistic Director; Julia C. Levy, Executive Director) at the Harold and Miriam Steinberg Center for Theatre on October 20, 2022. The performance was directed by David Mendizábal, with set design by Wilson Chin, costume design by Ásta Bennie Hostetter, lighting design by Nic Vincent, make-up design by Kirk Cambridge Del-Pesche, sound design and original music by Mauricio Escamilla, choreography by Tislarm Bouie, and fight direction and intimacy coordination by Rocío Mendez. The cast was as follows:

JONAH IRBY .... Jhardon Dishon Milton

GERALDINE IRBY .... Stephanie Berry

ELLA IRBY.......................... Sasha Manuel, Phoenix Noelle

SAM YATES .... Jake Ryan Lozano

RUBEN TORRES.............................Anthony Lee Medina

UNDERSTUDIES . . .Thursday Farrar, Preston Perez, Deon Releford-Lee

the bandaged place was originally presented by New York Stage and Film and Vassar in the Powerhouse Season, Summer 2019.

CHARACTERS

1 woman, 3 men, 1 child

JONAH IRBY – Black, Male-identifying, mid-20s/early 30s. Ella's biological father, but not her legal guardian. Recently injured and still a bit shell-shocked. *Dancer or strong mover.*

GERALDINE IRBY – Black, Female-identifying, early 60s. Jonah's grandmother and Ella's great-grandmother and legal guardian. Accustomed to holding things together.

ELLA IRBY – Black or Multi-racial, Female-identifying, 8 years old. Jonah's daughter. Wise beyond her years. *Dancer or strong mover.*

SAM YATES – Non-white, Male-identifying, mid-20s/early 30s. Ella's ballet teacher. A bit goofy. Stronger than he looks. *Dancer or strong mover.*

RUBEN TORRES – Black or Latine man, early/mid-30s. Jonah's ex-boyfriend. The kind of guy you don't say "no" to. Sexy as fuck.

SETTING

Jonah's studio apartment in Harlem
and various other locations around New York City

TIME

November 2006
Pre-iPhone

STYLE

The scenes should tumble

TIMELINE

Spring 1997
> Jonah and Q have sex after Junior Prom.

Spring 1998
> Ella is born.
> She is adopted by Geraldine.
> Jonah and Q graduate from high school.
> Q moves to California.

Fall 1998
> Jonah enters Juilliard.

Spring 2002
> Jonah graduates from Juilliard.
> He joins Ephemeral, a dance company based in Harlem.
> He lives with Geraldine and Ella.

January 2006
> Jonah meets Ruben on the street in the West Village.

February 2006
> Jonah moves in with Ruben in East New York.

Early September 2006
> Jonah is assaulted by Ruben.
> Jonah spends two nights in Jamaica Hospital then moves back in with Geraldine and Ella.

October 2006
> Jonah moves into his own apartment.

(From the dark:)

(A ringing phone.)

(Lights up on **JONAH** *asleep.)*

(Eventually, he stirs.)

(He answers the phone without checking the number.)

JONAH. hello?

(Beat.)

Hello –?

*(***RUBEN*** appears.)*

RUBEN. Hey.

*(***RUBEN**'s voice has an immediate effect on* **JONAH**.*)*

(He sits up, suddenly alert.)

Jonah?

(Beat.)

Boy, I can hear you breathing –

JONAH. How'd you get this number?

RUBEN. Phone book.

JONAH. Fuck you, how?

(Slight beat.)

Ruben, I said how?

RUBEN. *(Matter of fact.)* Does it matter?

    (Beat.)

JONAH. Yr not supposed to call.

RUBEN. Yeah, and yr not supposed to pick up, but here we are.

    (Beat.)

JONAH. What do you want?

RUBEN. What do I want? Seriously / J –?

JONAH. Yeah, seriously, what do you want –?

RUBEN. Hey, come on / now –

JONAH. It's a simple question, Ruben. What the *fuck* do you / want –?

RUBEN. Damn boy, all right, calm down! I don't want nothing!

JONAH. Bullshit.

RUBEN. Listen to you / nasty mouth –

JONAH. I'm hanging up, you hear? / I'm hanging up –!

RUBEN. Fuck, Jonah, WAIT, OKAY? SHIT!

    *(**RUBEN** collects himself.)*

I don't know why I called. My fingers just dialed yr number like they were on autopilot or something. I think they miss you.

    (Slight beat.)

Jonah?

    (Slight beat.)

Jonah, you hear me –?

JONAH. I can't do this.

RUBEN. What? Can't do what? Talk? You can't talk? You don't wanna talk –?

JONAH. No, that's not...

That's not what I mean and you know it.

You know.

> *(They breathe into their respective phones.* **RUBEN** *recalibrates.)*

RUBEN. I rewatched yr boy Woody's movie the other day. *Manhattan*? It was playing on TCM and I remembered how when we first started talking, you asked me if I'd seen it and I said no and you got all irate. / You remember that –?

JONAH. I wasn't irate –

RUBEN. You were like, "what do you mean you've never seen *Manhattan* –?"

JONAH. I don't sound like that –

RUBEN. And I was like, "I can't with Woody Allen." And you were like, "what are you talking about?" And I was like, "first of all would it kill him to put some color up on the screen –?"

JONAH. And I said, that's not his aesthetic –

RUBEN. And second, "does he have to be in all his own movies –?"

JONAH. He's not in all of them –

RUBEN. 'Cause I mean he kvetches like a pro, like a world-class champ for sure, but he can't act for shit –

JONAH. Okay, well, that's a matter of opinion –

RUBEN. And you were like, "you can't have lived in New York City yr whole damn life and not seen *Manhattan*, you know, 'cause it's like –"

RUBEN & JONAH. "A fucking love letter to New York."

> (**RUBEN** *smiles. He's got him.*)

RUBEN. You *do* remember.

> (*A moment.*)

I miss you, J.

I miss yr mouth.

Yr cute little ears.

Yr *ass* –

JONAH. Ruben –

RUBEN. And you miss me, too.

I know it.

I can hear it in yr voice.

The way you say my name.

Ruben –

JONAH. *Ruben* –

RUBEN. See there.

> (*Beat.*)

Yr the only one for me, Jonah.

I've said it from jump. From jump.

The only one.

You know that, right?

> (*Slight beat.*)

Come on, J –

> (**JONAH** *snaps his phone shut.*)

JONAH. Fuck.

Fuck, fuck, fuck, fuck, stupid, stupid, stupid.

Okay.

Just breathe.

Yr okay.

Yr gonna be –

> (**JONAH**'s *phone rings again.*)

You've gotta be fucking kidding me!

> (*He answers.*)

LEAVE ME THE FUCK ALONE!

> (**GERALDINE** *appears.*)

GERALDINE. EXCUSE ME?

JONAH. Aw, fuck –

GERALDINE. Jonah?

> (*Slight beat.*)

Boy, you better answer / me when I'm talking to you –

JONAH. Yes, Nana, I'm here / Shit –

GERALDINE. Is that how I taught you to answer the phone –?

JONAH. No, ma'am / no, ma'am –

GERALDINE. No, ma'am, is right. Answering the phone like you ain't got no sense. Like you ain't got no home / training –

JONAH. I'm sorry, okay? I didn't know it was you. I didn't *think* / it was you –

GERALDINE. Child, I know what you thought, *who* you thought I –

> (**GERALDINE** *recalibrates.*)

GERALDINE. You *do* understand he's not supposed to be calling you, right?

JONAH. Yes –

GERALDINE. That it's a condition of the restraining / order –

JONAH. Yes, I know –

GERALDINE. "No contact. No communication –"

JONAH. Nana, I said, I know! You've made yr point.

(*Slight beat.*)

GERALDINE. How did he get yr number?

JONAH. What?

GERALDINE. You heard me / how did he get –?

JONAH. I don't know –

GERALDINE. What do you mean / you don't know –?

JONAH. I mean, I don't know. He's... well, you know how he is. He's diabolical.

(*Beat.*)

GERALDINE. Does he know where yr living?

(*Slight beat.*)

Jonah Sebastian Irby, does that man know / where you live –?

JONAH. (*A tantrum.*) No, Nana / GOD –!

GERALDINE. Oh, okay now, okay. Don't be getting all attitudinal with me. It's not a crazy question. If he has yr phone number then it follows that he could have yr address. I'm worried about you.

JONAH. I'm fine, Nana / really –

GERALDINE. I hate that word. "Fine." It doesn't mean anything –

JONAH. What it means is I'm handling it. It means I'm good and I'm handling it.

GERALDINE. Yeah, well, I guess I'll just have to take yr word for it, won't I?

(Slight beat.)

Change yr number.

(Slight beat.)

Jonah –

JONAH. Yeah, okay / I will –

GERALDINE. And not tomorrow or next week. / *Today* –

JONAH. I said, I will –

GERALDINE. And keep it to yrself –

JONAH. *Nana!*

GERALDINE. Okay, okay, I'm done. Don't have to tell me twice.

(Slight beat.)

Lord, you got me all worked up and this isn't even why I called.

JONAH. *(With bite.)* Why did you?

> (**GERALDINE** *notes the attitude, but presses on without comment.*)

GERALDINE. I *called* to remind you that it's yr day to pick Ella up / from her dance class –

JONAH. *(Under his breath.)* Aw, shit –

> (**JONAH** *begins to dress. Pulling on pants, socks, shoes, etc. It takes a while.*)

GERALDINE. Which I thought might be appropriate given yr "variable" schedule –

JONAH. *(Under his breath.)* Shit, shit, shit –

GERALDINE. Jonah, are you hearing me?

JONAH. Yes, Nana, I hear you –

GERALDINE. Because I'm leaving for my meeting at the church in five minutes and I need to know if that plan needs to change.

> *(Slight beat.)*

Jonah?

> *(Slight beat.)*

Jonah, what the hell is going on over there?

JONAH. Nothing. Go to yr meeting.

GERALDINE. Boy, are you still in bed?

JONAH. What? Uh / no –

GERALDINE. Jonah, we have talked about this. You cannot stay in bed all day. / Life goes on, baby –

JONAH. I'm not still –

I know that life –

Fuck!

GERALDINE. Language!

JONAH. Sorry!

> *(They breathe into their respective phones.)*

GERALDINE. Now I'm not trying to be all up in yr business / or anything –

JONAH. Oh no –?

GERALDINE. But it's been a month. A month of you holed up in that apartment telling me yr fine when I know yr not fine –

JONAH. Nana –

GERALDINE. And avoiding yr daughter

Which

Okay

Do me however you wanna do me

Screen my calls, whatever, I can take it, I'm an adult, but her?

Jonah, she's a child –

JONAH. I know what she is –

GERALDINE. And she needs her father –

JONAH. *You don't think I know that?*

(*They breathe into their respective phones.*)

GERALDINE. Look, all I need to know is if yr gonna pick Ella up from class or if I need to cancel my meeting.

(*Slight beat.*)

Boy –!

JONAH. No, don't cancel. I'm on it, okay? I'm on it.

(**JONAH** *closes his phone. He collects his wallet and his cane. He moves to the door and unlocks it – all three locks. One last breath and then –*)

I. Am. On it.

(**JONAH** *exits.*)

(*His apartment falls away. Outside of dance class.* **SAM** *waits with* **ELLA**.)

ELLA. My nana has a hat lady meeting so my daddy is picking me up.

SAM. Well, I'm sure he's on his way.

ELLA. Yeah, only sometimes he oversleeps. Like on Sundays when he's supposed to come to church. He always says, "sorry, I forgot to set my alarm," but I think he forgets on purpose. He believes in God though. Nana says that just because a person doesn't go to church doesn't mean they don't like God. She says that God loves everybody. Even people who don't go to church. Do you go to church, Mr. Sam?

SAM. Um... / What –?

ELLA. We're Baptists. That's the name of the de-nomination. Baptist. There are lots of different de-nominations. Methodists, Southern Baptists, Presbyterians, Evangelicals, Pentecostals... They like fire.

SAM. Do you think we should try calling yr father?

ELLA. We could. Only he's got Sprint so he doesn't get service underground. Do you have Sprint?

SAM. Uh, no. AT&T / but –

ELLA. Oh, that's way better. Less dropped calls.

(**ELLA** *dances around.* **SAM** *recalibrates.*)

SAM. Do you know his phone number?

ELLA. Yep.

(**ELLA** *continues to dance.*)

SAM. Um, well, would you mind telling it to me / so that I can call him –?

ELLA. Oh yeah!

(**ELLA** *moves to* **SAM.**)

It's three four seven four three two three five seven four.

(**SAM** *types in the number. He shows the screen to* **ELLA** *who confirms with a thumbs up.* **ELLA** *dances around and with* **SAM** *as he leaves his message.*)

JONAH'S CELL PHONE. *(Pre-recorded.)* "The person at the number you have dialed is not available.

Please leave a message after the tone."

(A beep.)

SAM. *(No cause for alarm.)* Um, hi, Mr. Irby?

This is Sam Yates from Alvin Ailey.

I'm here with Ella.

And, well, um... class ended almost twenty minutes ago and I'm just calling to make sure that someone, she says you, is on the way to pick her up –

(**JONAH** *appears.*)

ELLA. Daddy!

JONAH. Hey, Belly.

(**ELLA** *crashes into her father.*)

Ooo careful.

ELLA. Daddy, yr late.

JONAH. I know.

ELLA. I'm the last person left. I'm even later than Serafina and her mom is always late. Right, Mr. Sam?

SAM. Well...

ELLA. See, Daddy, "well" means yes.

JONAH. I'm sorry.

ELLA. Yr forgiven.

JONAH. Thank you.

> (**ELLA** *drags* **SAM** *toward her father.*)

ELLA. Daddy, this is my teacher, Mr. Sam.

SAM. Hi.

> (**SAM** *extends his hand.* **JONAH** *flinches slightly, then offers his own. They shake.*)

JONAH. Hey. Jonah.

SAM. Nice to meet you.

ELLA. *(To* **SAM**.*)* The last time my daddy picked me up from dance class I was only in Level Two. Now I'm in Level Three.

JONAH. They grow up so fast.

SAM. That they do.

ELLA. Daddy, see what I learned today?

> (**ELLA** *demonstrates.* **JONAH** *and* **SAM** *watch her dance.*)

JONAH. I'm sorry I'm late. Ella's grandmother usually handles pick up.

SAM. Geraldine.

JONAH. Yeah, Geraldine.

SAM. She's a force.

JONAH. She's definitely something.

> (*Slight beat.*)

Ella loves yr class, by the way. She talks about it constantly.

SAM. Well, I love having her. She's a very talented little girl.

JONAH. I bet you say that to all the parents.

SAM. I do. But in this case, it's true.

ELLA. Daddy, did you see me? Did you see?!

JONAH. I did, I did. You looked wonderful.

ELLA. Did he really watch, Mr. Sam?

SAM. Oh, totally. He didn't blink once.

ELLA. *(To* **JONAH.***)* You didn't?

JONAH. I was like this the whole time.

> *(***JONAH*** makes a funny face.)*

ELLA. Whatever, Daddy.

> *(***ELLA*** moves to her dance bag. She puts on her coat, scarf, hat, etc.)*

SAM. Ella mentioned that you dance, too.

JONAH. She did?

SAM. She did. Are you with a company or...?

JONAH. Uh yeah, I'm with Eve Grant? Up in Harlem?

SAM. Wait. Ephemeral?

JONAH. You know it?

SAM. Are you kidding? I saw you guys perform at The Joyce last Spring. You were incredible. *The Times* loves you.

JONAH. They've been kind.

SAM. Effusive is more like it. And totally deserved. In my humble humble opinion.

> *(A shared smile.)*

Is it a rehearsal injury?

JONAH. *(A lie.)* Oh. Uh... yeah.

SAM. How bad?

JONAH. Just a sprain.

SAM. Still... ouch.

JONAH. Yeah...

SAM. I tore my ACL a couple years ago playing volleyball in Central Park and I was off my feet for nine months. I almost went crazy.

JONAH. I know the feeling.

SAM. And like all I wanted to do was dance. Like the whole time. And even after the doctor cleared me, I'd try, you know, and... chicken out. Like I'd start a phrase, and then...

>   *(Beat.)*

Anyway, it's intense stuff.

JONAH. Totally.

>   *(Slight beat.)*

SAM. You know, if yr looking for a therapist, I had a really great one.

JONAH. Thanks. But I'm good.

>   (**ELLA** *crosses to* **JONAH**. *She hands him her bag.)*

ELLA. Daddy! I'm hungry!

JONAH. I guess she's hungry.

ELLA. Come on!

SAM. And I guess yr going.

ELLA. Bye, Mr. Sam.

>   (**ELLA** *exits.)*

SAM. Bye, Ella. See you Wednesday.

JONAH. Thanks again for waiting –

ELLA. *(Offstage.)* DADDY!

JONAH. Coming!

SAM. You'd better go catch yr kid.

JONAH. Right. Well, um... bye.

SAM. See ya.

> *(Mount Morris Park materializes.* **ELLA** *holds a hotdog.)*

JONAH. So...?

ELLA. *(Sing-song.)* "So, so, suck yr toe, all the way to Mexico."

JONAH. Yr good then?

ELLA. Yeah, I'm good, Nana's good, everybody's good.

JONAH. Well, good.

ELLA. Are you?

JONAH. Yeah, of course.

> *(***ELLA** *looks at her father's cane.* **JONAH** *sees his daughter looking at his cane.)*

What? Do I not look good? Is it my hair?

ELLA. No, Daddy. Yr hair looks fine.

> *(***ELLA** *takes a bite of her hotdog.)*

Mmm, I love hotdogs! Nana never lets me have them.

JONAH. She wouldn't let me have them either when I was yr age. She would say, "little boy."

> *(***ELLA** *laughs at his impersonation.)*

"Little boy, you can't imagine the shit they put in those things."

(Crap, he just said "shit.")

JONAH. Oh, fuck.

(Shit, he just said "fuck." **ELLA** *laughs harder.)*

Ella, I –

ELLA. It's okay, Daddy. I've heard bad words before. Lots of times.

JONAH. Please don't tell Nana –

ELLA. I won't –

JONAH. About the hotdogs or the / bad words –

ELLA. I said I won't, Daddy.

JONAH. Pinkie swear.

*(***JONAH*** offers his pinkie finger.)*

ELLA. You know, no one pinkie swears anymore, right?

JONAH. *We* do.

(A moment and then **ELLA** *smiles, then pinkie swears with her father.)*

ELLA. Yeah. We do.

(Geraldine's entryway materializes.)

GERALDINE. Did you have fun?

*(***ELLA*** moves to* **GERALDINE** *and hugs her.)*

ELLA. Uh huh. We went to the park.

GERALDINE. *(A scold to* **JONAH**.*)* As cold as it is out there?

ELLA. Daddy made me wear my scarf –

JONAH. And yr hat –

ELLA. *And* my hat –

GERALDINE. Well, I should hope so.

(*To* **JONAH.**) Were you very late picking her up?

JONAH. No, not very.

ELLA. And besides it was okay because Mr. Sam waited with me and he doesn't mind. I think I'm his favorite.

GERALDINE. Oh, you do, do you?

ELLA. Uh huh. Did you know he has AT&T?

GERALDINE. I did not.

ELLA. Yep. "More bars in more places."

GERALDINE. Little girl, what do you know about "bars"?

ELLA. Everybody knows about bars, Nana. Everybody!

GERALDINE. (*To* **JONAH.**) Do you hear yr child?

JONAH. You mean this loud thing right here?

ELLA. I'm not loud!

JONAH. This "know it all" right here?

ELLA. Daddy!   **GERALDINE.** That's exactly the one!

(**GERALDINE** *turns to* **ELLA.**)

GERALDINE. Why don't you take yr things upstairs and put them where you *know* they go.

ELLA. Yes, ma'am.

(*To* **JONAH.**) Daddy, are you staying for dinner?

(**JONAH** *looks at* **GERALDINE** *and then* –)

JONAH. We'll see.

ELLA. Don't leave 'til I get back!

(**ELLA** *exits.*)

(*A moment and then* –)

GERALDINE. You look thin.

JONAH. You say that every time you see me.

GERALDINE. And every time I see you it's true. Are you eating?

JONAH. Of course, I'm eating. People gotta eat.

GERALDINE. Something other than McDonald's?

(*Slight beat.*)

Jonah –

JONAH. Does pizza count?

GERALDINE. Lord, help me. Anything green?

JONAH. Olives?

GERALDINE. Very funny.

(*Beat.*)

How's the apartment?

JONAH. It's good.

GERALDINE. The stairs aren't giving you trouble?

JONAH. Nah.

(*She gestures to his knee.*)

I swear, Nana. I'm fine.

GERALDINE. There's that word again.

JONAH. Sorry.

GERALDINE. Are you still seeing that therapist?

(**JONAH** *is not still seeing the therapist.*)

I paid for three months, Jonah.

JONAH. I know –

GERALDINE. *Three –*

JONAH. I said, I know.

GERALDINE. You need to talk to someone.

JONAH. I do. I am.

GERALDINE. Who? Who do you talk to?

JONAH. You don't know everyone I know.

(*And then with renewed vigor –*)

GERALDINE. You need to take care of yrself –

JONAH. I am –

GERALDINE. Go to those appointments. Get out more. Come to dinner –

JONAH. And there it is! The dinner invitation.

GERALDINE. It's easy, Jonah. Dinner is easy. You come inside the house. You sit at the table. You spend time with yr daughter. You eat. Maybe spend the night. Yr room's still up there –

JONAH. Yeah, I've gotta go.

GERALDINE. Little boy, you grew up in this house, running all up and down these halls, slamming these doors. I don't understand why getting you to come in past the entryway is such an ordeal –

JONAH. It's not an ordeal, I just –

GERALDINE. You just what?

JONAH. Can't, all right. I just can't –

GERALDINE. (*Exasperated.*) What does that even mean?

(*Beat.*)

JONAH. Will you please tell Ella that / I –

GERALDINE. That you love her and that yr sorry you couldn't stay. Yeah, I know.

> (**JONAH** *exits.*)

> (*A moment and then –*)

> (**ELLA** *returns.*)

ELLA. All put away!

GERALDINE. Very good!

ELLA. Where's Daddy?

GERALDINE. He had to go.

ELLA. But he said, we'll see.

GERALDINE. I know and he felt terrible, but he left you hugs and kisses. Do you want 'em?

ELLA. Yes.

> (**GERALDINE** *hugs and kisses* **ELLA***.*)

GERALDINE. Did you wash up for dinner?

ELLA. Uh huh. Both hands.

GERALDINE. *(With a chuckle.)* I didn't realize there was a one-handed option.

ELLA. Oh, there is.

GERALDINE. Well, I guess it is true what they say. You learn something new every day. Go set the table for dinner. Food's almost ready.

ELLA. Okay, but you should know, I'm not very hungry.

GERALDINE. What do you mean, yr not hungry? Little girl, yr always hungry –

ELLA. Yeah, but me and Daddy had hotdogs in the park and –

> (*She just spilled the secret.*)

Oops!

GERALDINE. Uh huh. Oops is right.

> *(Later that night.)*
>
> *(Jonah's apartment materializes.)*
>
> *(He enters, listening to music with earphones.)*
>
> (**JONAH** *empties the contents of a laundry bag onto the bed and begins to fold.)*
>
> *(One item triggers a memory.)*
>
> (**RUBEN** *appears.)*
>
> *(He watches* **JONAH** *for a moment, then moves closer and playfully smacks his ass.)*
>
> (**JONAH** *removes his earphones.)*

JONAH. Hey! Sorry, I didn't know you were home.

RUBEN. I love how you do that.

JONAH. How I do what?

RUBEN. Fold everything up like we live in a department store. Like we live in the Gap.

JONAH. I ain't studying the Gap.

RUBEN. Yeah, yr right, yr right. Yr more of a Banana Republic kinda guy. Upscale.

JONAH. I'm not upscale.

> (**RUBEN** *gives* **JONAH** *a look.)*

What, I'm not!

RUBEN. Yeah, okay, whatever you say.

> *(Slight beat.)*

Bougie ass bitch.

JONAH. Hey!

>   (**RUBEN** *laughs.*)

You be nice to me! I'm folding yr fucking underwear!

>   (*Slight beat.*)

Jerk.

RUBEN. You love it.

JONAH. You *think* I love it.

>   (**JONAH** *returns to folding.* **RUBEN** *watches.*)

RUBEN. Hey, stop for a minute.

JONAH. Nah, I'm almost finished –

RUBEN. Just stop.

JONAH. Ruben –

RUBEN. I got you something.

JONAH. You...? You what?

RUBEN. Close yr eyes and hold out yr hand.

JONAH. You know I hate surprises –

RUBEN. Boy, just close yr eyes!

>   (**JONAH** *hesitates.*)

What, you don't trust me?

JONAH. Nuh-uh.

RUBEN. Come on now. Do as I say.

>   (*Slight beat.*)

Well, come on –

JONAH. Fine.

*(**JONAH** closes his eyes.)*

RUBEN. Gimme yr hand.

*(**JONAH** holds out his hand. **RUBEN** produces a box and sets it in **JONAH**'s open palm.)*

And... open.

*(**JONAH** opens his eyes.)*

JONAH. Aw, you got me a box!

RUBEN. Bitch, open it!

*(**JONAH** does. He removes a gold chain from the box.)*

Now I know yr not the chain-wearing type, but yr living in East New York now and ain't nobody out here gonna know yr taken unless yr wearing something on yr finger or around yr neck.

*(**RUBEN** clasps the chain around **JONAH**'s neck.)*

There. What do you think?

*(**JONAH** fingers the chain.)*

You hate it.

JONAH. No.

RUBEN. You do / you do –

JONAH. I don't / Ruben –

RUBEN. *(Sudden, violent.)* Fuck, I knew / it was a mistake –!

JONAH. Babe, I like it, okay? I like it!

RUBEN. You do?

JONAH. Yeah, I do.

RUBEN. For real? 'Cause I can take it back –

(**JONAH** *kisses* **RUBEN** *to shut him up.*)

JONAH. Thank you.

RUBEN. Yr welcome.

(*They kiss again, more intensely. Eventually,* **JONAH** *pulls away.*)

JONAH. Now go away and let me finish folding.

RUBEN. *(Suggestive.)* Or I could stay and fold you instead.

(**JONAH** *swats* **RUBEN** *with an article of clothing.*)

JONAH. Go!

RUBEN. Yeah, all right. Later though? I'ma tear that ass up.

(**RUBEN** *disappears.*)

(**JONAH** *fingers the chain around his neck.*)

(**GERALDINE** *appears.*)

(*She flips open her phone and dials a number.*)

(**JONAH**'*s phone rings.*)

(*He checks the number...*)

JONAH. Nuh-uh.

(*...and ignores her call.*)

JONAH'S CELL PHONE. *(Pre-recorded.)* "The person at the number you have dialed is not available.
Please leave a message after the tone."

(*A beep.*)

GERALDINE. Boy, do you ever pick up yr phone!

(*She sighs.*)

Anyway,

I'm calling because Ella wanted to know if you could pick her up from dance on Wednesday.

I told her I wasn't sure of yr schedule, but that I would ask, so I'm asking.

Class ends at six thirty.

Six thirty.

S-I-X thirty.

You hear me?

Children need a schedule, Jonah.

They need stability.

A routine.

Let me know if yr free.

OH

And I heard about those hotdogs.

You know that little girl can't keep a secret.

Jonah, you need to learn to practice restraint.

Just because something looks good, smells good or even tastes good, does not mean that it is good for you.

Shit, those things are filled with pig lips and anuses.

Do you hear me?

Pig lips and anuses!

Restraint, Jonah.

Restraint!

Anyway,

Let me know about Wednesday.

You can text me if you must.

GERALDINE. You know how I feel about texts, but –

You know what?

Let me stop.

Call me back, okay?

Love, Grandma.

> (**GERALDINE** *closes her phone.*)
>
> (*Wednesday.*)
>
> (*After ballet class.*)
>
> (**ELLA** *sits, legs pulled to her chest.*)
>
> (*She wears men's boxer shorts.*)

SAM. I left messages for yr grandmother and yr father. Is there anyone else I can call? A neighbor maybe? Yr mom?

ELLA. I don't have a mom.

SAM. Oh, um, I didn't... I'm sorry.

ELLA. It's okay.

> (*A moment and then* **SAM** *sits next to* **ELLA.***)*

SAM. You know, when I was just a little older than you, I went to this amusement park with my brother and his friends. And they were all in middle school and I was in like the fifth grade and they were all going on the roller coasters. Have you ever been on a roller coaster?

> (**ELLA** *shakes her head no.*)

Yeah, well neither had I and I really wanted to, mostly because I wanted to prove to my brother that I could, you know? To prove that I could handle a big kid ride. Anyway, I was too young and too short –

ELLA. (*Dismissive.*) So you couldn't go.

SAM. So I couldn't go.

> *(**SAM** recalibrates.)*

But there was this other ride that I could go on called the Gravitron.

ELLA. The Gravitron?

SAM. Yeah, the Gravitron.

ELLA. What's that?

SAM. Well, it was this ride where you stood against a wall and they strapped you in –

ELLA. To the wall?

SAM. To the wall and then...

> *(**SAM** pulls **ELLA** to her feet and spins her around.)*

...it would spin like really superfast and then the floor would fall away and yr body would stick to the wall and there'd be nothing below yr feet.

ELLA. That doesn't sound very fun.

SAM. Well, as it turns out, it wasn't. Mostly, it just made me sick. Very, very, sick. And while we were spinning – me, my brother and my brother's friends... I barfed.

ELLA. You...?

> *(**SAM** demonstrates.)*

Ew gross, Mr. Sam!

SAM. Yeah, it was pretty gross. It actually might be the grossest thing that's ever happened to me.

> *(He shudders.)*

Anyway, my brother was pissed – *mad.* My brother was *mad* and his friends were *mad* and everyone on the ride was *mad* because, of course, they were covered in –

ELLA. Barf.

SAM. Right, barf. And I was mortified. I literally wanted to crawl under a rock and disappear, but, and this is the important thing, I didn't. I survived.

> *(Slight beat.)*

I guess what I'm saying is that embarrassing things happen. To some of us – *me* – they happen all the time and it's okay. It'll be okay.

> *(Beat.)*

Anyway...

> *(A moment and then* **ELLA** *hugs* **SAM**. **JONAH** *appears with his cane.)*

JONAH. Sorry, sorry, I got stuck underground and...

> *(***JONAH** *takes in the scene.)*

What happened?

SAM. Everything's fine.

JONAH. Ella, where are yr clothes?

SAM. Um can we speak privately?

JONAH. Uh –

SAM. Just over here?

JONAH. Uh, yeah, sure.

SAM. Ella, I'm just gonna chat with yr dad for a minute.

ELLA. Okay.

SAM. Mr. Irby –

JONAH. What's going on? Why is she in boxers?

SAM. She wet herself.

JONAH. She / what –?

SAM. One of the mothers cleaned her up. I think she got a little overwhelmed in class –

JONAH. What do you mean overwhelmed? What were you doing in class that was so / overwhelming –?

SAM. Mr. Irby, I think for Ella's sake we should try to keep our voices down. There's no need to further traumatize –

JONAH. Traumatize –!

SAM. She's embarrassed. Understandably. I mean, everyone saw – the other kids, the other mothers, me...

(Slight beat.)

I left a message for Geraldine –

JONAH. You... shit / No –

SAM. I'm sorry, but you weren't / here –

JONAH. The train stalled. Fuck.

SAM. I was very clear in my message that this was no one's fault.

JONAH. Yeah, well, that's not the way she'll see it.

SAM. *(Treading carefully, but unapologetically.)* Um... okay, so I don't mean to overstep. And please, stop me if I do, but I've been doing this for a long time, working with kids, and I've learned a few things. First and foremost, if you say yr gonna be somewhere then you've gotta be there. On time. Yr kid needs to know that if and when something happens, and things do happen, yr gonna be right there to make it better.

JONAH. I can't control the MTA –

SAM. You don't owe me an explanation. I'm just... this is just what I see. Ella is pretty incredible. She's bright and poised and talented and she has a good heart.

ELLA. Daddy, can we go home now?

SAM. She doesn't have anything to be ashamed of.

JONAH. Of course, Belly.

> (**JONAH** *hands* **ELLA** *off to* **GERALDINE** *as her brownstone materializes.*)

ELLA. Nana, have you ever been on the Gravitron?

GERALDINE. The what-a-tron?

ELLA. The Gravitron.

GERALDINE. Little girl, what are you talking about?

ELLA. It's this ride where you spin superfast and then the floor goes away and then you stick to the wall.

GERALDINE. It sounds terrifying.

ELLA. It made Mr. Sam sick. He barfed all over everybody.

GERALDINE. Ella.

ELLA. What? He did.

> (**GERALDINE** *gives* **ELLA** *a look.*)

What?

GERALDINE. We don't say barf.

ELLA. Why not?

GERALDINE. Because it's inappropriate.

ELLA. But why?

GERALDINE. Because vomit isn't an appropriate topic for polite conversation.

> (**ELLA** *considers this and then–*)

ELLA. I think vomit sounds even grosser than barf.

Vomit!

Vomit!

Vomit!

Vomit-o –!

GERALDINE. All right now –

ELLA. Vomit!

Vomit –!

GERALDINE. Go take a bath, go on –

ELLA. Vomit!

Vomit!

Vomit –

> (**ELLA** *pretends to barf on* **GERALDINE.***)*

GERALDINE. Ella!

> (*An immediate correction.*)

ELLA. Yes, ma'am!

> (**ELLA** *exits.*)

> (**GERALDINE** *follows.*)

> (**JONAH** *appears.*)

> (*He begins to move.*)

> (*He stretches, at first.*)

> (*And then, simple motions, gestures – a turn of the head, a wave of a hand.*)

> (*The effect is one of cumulative beauty.*)

> (*After a while,* **RUBEN** *appears.*)

> (**JONAH** *starts to bend his knee.*)

> (*He hesitates.*)

JONAH. Shit.

(He tries, again. Again, he hesitates.)

JONAH. Fuck.

> (**JONAH** *breathes, frustrated. With himself, with his body.)*

Okay.

Just breathe.

Yr okay.

Yr gonna be –

(He tries, again. Hesitation.)

What the fuck!

(He turns to **RUBEN**.*)*

Go away!

RUBEN. You remember our first time?

JONAH. What? No.

RUBEN. Yeah, you do. That squeaky sofa at my mom's? Everybody heard us. Everybody. Osvaldo. The neighbors. I love that you turned out to be a screamer.

JONAH. Ruben.

RUBEN. What?

JONAH. Shut up.

RUBEN. Hey, what's true is true. You can't help the way you are.

JONAH. God, I miss you.

I know I'm not supposed to, but...

I miss yr fingers.

RUBEN. Yeah?

JONAH. Yeah.

RUBEN. What else?

(*Slight beat.*)

Come on now, J.

You know you don't have to be shy with me.

What else?

Tell Benny.

JONAH. I miss yr smell.

RUBEN. Yeah?

JONAH. Yeah, yr smell.

And yr mouth.

And yr tongue.

I miss yr body.

RUBEN. Yeah?

JONAH. I miss yr body when it's with my body.

Fuck, I sound like an e.e. cummings poem.

RUBEN. What else do you miss?

JONAH. It's like…

RUBEN. Yeah?

JONAH. It's like yr in my bloodstream. It's like yr coursing through my veins and I know I'm not supposed to want you. I know that I'm supposed to want you out, but –

(**RUBEN**'s *hand disappears down* **JONAH**'s *pants.* **JONAH** *gasps.*)

RUBEN. Do you miss that?

JONAH. I, uh… yeah.

RUBEN. Yeah?

JONAH. Yeah. Yeah, I do.

RUBEN. Tell me you like it.

Come on, J.

Tell me you like it.

JONAH. I like it.

RUBEN. Yeah?

JONAH. Yeah.

RUBEN. Yeah, I know.

Benny knows what you like.

> (**RUBEN** *disappears, but* **JONAH***'s hand persists.)*

> *(He's been alone the whole time.)*

JONAH. Oh god.

Oh god, yes.

Yes.

Yes.

Fuck.

Oh fuck.

Oh shit.

OH SHIT.

HOLY –

> *(A release.)*

> *(Monday.)*

> *(Dance class.)*

*(**SAM** and **ELLA** do a routine.)*

*(**JONAH** appears, applauding.)*

(He does not have his cane.)

ELLA. Daddy!

JONAH. Hey, Belly.

> *(**ELLA** hugs her father, gentler than the last time.)*

ELLA. Yr on time.

JONAH. Miracles do happen, right?

ELLA. Mr. Sam, look who's here!

SAM. I see. Hi again.

JONAH. Hi.

ELLA. "Marked improvement," huh?

SAM. Definitely "gold star" worthy.

JONAH. Thank you.

ELLA. We should celebrate with hotdogs!

JONAH. I don't think that would make yr grandmother very happy.

ELLA. I won't tell her this time, I promise.

JONAH. Not today, Belly. I'm sure she's already hard at work on dinner.

ELLA. For all of us?

JONAH. Well, for you.

ELLA. Can Mr. Sam come?

JONAH. Can / he –?

ELLA. Come to dinner?

JONAH. Oh.

ELLA. You can both come.

SAM. Oh, no, Ella / That's –   **JONAH.** Belly, I don't think
                                   / that's a good idea –

ELLA. *(To* **JONAH.***)* Why not? It's almost dinner time and
he looks hungry.

Aren't you hungry, Mr. Sam?

SAM. Um...

> *(He looks to* **JONAH.***)*

Not really?

JONAH. Ella, it's very kind of you to invite Sam, but I'm
sure he already has plans –

ELLA. *(To* **SAM.***)* Do you?

JONAH. Ella.

SAM. Do I...?

ELLA. Have plans?

SAM. Well, um...

ELLA. See, Daddy. "well, um" means no.

JONAH. I –

ELLA. Please.

> *(***JONAH** *takes a breath then turns to* **SAM.***)*

JONAH. Sam, would you like to join us for dinner? My
daughter insists.

ELLA. Just say yes, Mr. Sam –

JONAH. Ella –

SAM. I'd love to.

ELLA. Yes!

SAM. Just give me five minutes to grab my stuff.

ELLA. Take yr time!

(**SAM** *exits.* **JONAH** *gives* **ELLA** *a look.*)

What? He did look hungry!

(*Grealdine's brownstone materializes.*)

(*A dining room table and chairs appear.*)

Mr. Sam, do you wanna see my room?

GERALDINE. Ella –

ELLA. After dinner, I mean. I mean, after dinner.

JONAH. Yr in for a real treat. It's a pretty great room.

ELLA. It's the best room. All my friends say so.

SAM. I can't wait.

(**ELLA** *shovels food into her mouth.*)

GERALDINE. Little girl, chew   **JONAH.** Belly, come on,
yr food! Don't act out just   slow down –
because we've got company.

ELLA. Yes, ma'am.

SAM. Everything was delicious, Mrs. Irby.

GERALDINE. Please. Call me, Geraldine.

SAM. Geraldine. I don't know what you did to that chicken, but it was out of this world.

GERALDINE. I'm glad you liked it. There's plenty more so help yrself to seconds.

ELLA. Nana always makes too much food.

JONAH. Ella –

ELLA. What? She does. Even when it's just us.

GERALDINE. I've never really gotten used to cooking for two. In fact, I had to get a second icebox for the overflow.

ELLA. We call him Billy Eckstine.

SAM. Wait, the freezer?

ELLA. Yeah, 'cause they're both so *cool.*

GERALDINE. You know, Sam, back in the day we used to have what we called "leftover parties."

ELLA. Did somebody say party?

> (**ELLA** *slides from her chair and dances around the dining room.*)

JONAH. Okay, Ella. That's enough.

> (**ELLA** *continues.* **JONAH** *moves to her, trying to entice her back to the table.*)

Ella, come back to the table.

> (**ELLA** *continues.*)

Ella, would you please –?

GERALDINE. Ella.

> (**ELLA** *sits immediately.*)

> (**JONAH**, *embarrassed, makes his way back to the table.*)

SAM. (*Attempting to smooth things over.*) Sorry, I'm not familiar with leftover parties.

GERALDINE. It's nothing really. We would have a few friends over, you know, folks from the neighborhood, and I would defrost everything and set it out and we'd eat and drink and socialize.

ELLA. I want to have a leftover party, Nana. Can we?

GERALDINE. It's a tradition, actually. My mother used to throw them and my grandmother before her. I don't know if my grandson told you this, but our family has lived in this brownstone for almost one hundred years.

(**ELLA** *yawns loudly.*)

Of course, some of us aren't quite old enough to appreciate history yet.

ELLA. I appreciate it. I just don't get why it has to be so boring. Can we go upstairs now?

GERALDINE. Is there still food on yr plate?

(*Again,* **ELLA** *shovels food into her mouth.*)

GERALDINE. Little girl, what did I say about chewing –?   **JONAH.** Ella, seriously –?

ELLA. All done!

(*She holds up her plate triumphantly.*)

Now can we go?

GERALDINE. (*With a sigh.*) Yes, now you may go.

ELLA. Finally!

GERALDINE. But we're going to have a talk about yr table manners later.

ELLA. Yes, ma'am. Come on, Mr. Sam. My room is this way!

SAM. Wish me luck.

JONAH. Good luck.

(**ELLA** *and* **SAM** *exit.*)

GERALDINE. Oh, and no jumping on the bed!

(*Slight beat.*)

Ella, do you hear me?

ELLA. *(Offstage.)* Yes, ma'am!

> (**GERALDINE** *laughs.*)

GERALDINE. Lord, that girl has so much energy.

JONAH. Yes, she does.

GERALDINE. Reminds me of you at that age. Flitting around every which way…

> *(Beat.)*

It was a nice surprise, you coming to dinner. And I'm glad you brought Sam. Ella came running in here screaming, "Nana, guess who's coming to dinner!" He's such a nice boy. So polite.

> *(Slight beat.)*

Was the food okay?

JONAH. You know it was.

GERALDINE. Yeah, I know, but I still like to ask. I did put my foot in that chicken tonight, if I do say so myself.

JONAH. You really did.

> (**JONAH** *smiles with teeth.*)

GERALDINE. Now see, that's what I loved most about tonight. You let yrself smile a few times.

JONAH. I smile.

GERALDINE. Boy, I could count on one hand the number of times I've seen yr teeth in the last month! I remember you were the smilingest baby…

JONAH. *(Embarrassed.)* Oh my god…

GERALDINE. You came out grinning from ear to ear. I remember I used to say to yr mother –

> (**GERALDINE** *stops herself. She begins to clear the table.*)

Anyway, I approve of Sam. Not that you need my approval.

JONAH. What did you say to her?

GERALDINE. Hm?

JONAH. To Mom. What did you used to say?

GERALDINE. Oh, I don't know Jonah. It was a long time ago. I don't remember every little thing that happened back then.

JONAH. We never talk about her.

GERALDINE. Who?

JONAH. Mom.

GERALDINE. What do you mean we never –? Of course, we do.

JONAH. Nah, we don't. We never do 'cause *you* never want to.

(*Slight beat.*)

Do you think I'm like her?

GERALDINE. What kind of question is that? Of course, yr like her. Yr her son.

JONAH. You know what I mean.

(*Beat.*)

You do. You think I am.

GERALDINE. I don't think this is the time or the place for this conversation.

JONAH. 'Cause you don't want to have it.

GERALDINE. No, because there's a little girl upstairs. Not to mention a guest. Restraint, Jonah / You need to learn to practice restraint –

JONAH. Bullshit. Bull. Shit –

GERALDINE. Excuse me?

JONAH. This has nothing to do with Ella or restraint –

GERALDINE. Little boy, you have so much to learn. That little girl upstairs is everything!

JONAH. Mom left because of you. You get that, right? She left *me* because she couldn't stand *you.*

(**GERALDINE** *makes a decision.*)

GERALDINE. Yr mother never figured out how to stand on her own two feet. She let herself be seduced by all manner of... Shay was self-destructive. End of story.

JONAH. Like me –

GERALDINE. That is not what I said –

JONAH. But that's what you think / That I'm self-destructive –

GERALDINE. I think, Jonah, I think that you have made choices.

JONAH. You mean, Ruben –

GERALDINE. I mean, choices. We all make / choices –

JONAH. You mean like Ruben –!

GERALDINE. OKAY, FINE. YES, I MEAN LIKE RUBEN!

(**JONAH** *fingers the chain at his neck.* **RUBEN** *appears.*)

Do you remember the night he came to dinner? He sat right there in that chair. And I saw the way he held onto yr shoulder, to yr thigh, like he was never letting you go.

(**RUBEN** *sits at the table.*)

And I knew. I knew then and there that he was trouble.

JONAH. You couldn't have known that!

GERALDINE. Don't you *ever* presume to know what I know! I sat there that night. History repeating itself at my table / and I –

ELLA. Daddy?

    *(**ELLA** and **SAM** have appeared.)*

SAM. I'm sorry. Ella heard voices / and –

ELLA. You were yelling.

GERALDINE. Ella, yr father and I were just having a conversation.

ELLA. It didn't sound like a conversation.

JONAH. Sam, we should go.

ELLA. Daddy, no!

JONAH. It's getting late and you still have homework.

ELLA. Just a worksheet! Stay!

GERALDINE. Ella, if yr father / feels –

JONAH. Nana, I am fully capable of talking to my daughter without yr help.

    *(To **ELLA**.)* Give me a hug.

    *(**ELLA** turns away from **JONAH**.)*

Ella.

    (Beat.)

Ella, please...

    *(Finally, **ELLA** embraces her father.)*

I love you so much.

ELLA. If you love me then stay.

JONAH. I wish it was that simple.

ELLA. It is, Daddy, it is!

(**ELLA** *latches onto* **JONAH***'s leg.*)

GERALDINE. Ella, let go of yr father.

ELLA. I don't wanna!

GERALDINE. Ella –

JONAH. Belly, I know yr upset, but Daddy has to go.

ELLA. *(The beginning of a tantrum.)* NO!

JONAH. Ella –

ELLA. I'm not letting go
    I'm not letting go
    I'm not letting go
    I'm not letting go   **GERALDINE.** Ella Fitzgerald
    I'm not letting go   Irby, let go right now.
    I'm not letting go
    I'm not letting go
    I'm not letting go   **JONAH.** Ella, my knee.
    I'm not letting go
    I'm not letting go
    I'm not letting go   **GERALDINE.** Don't make me
    I'm not letting go   pull you off.
    I'm not letting go
    I'm not letting go   **JONAH.** Ella, that hurts.
    I'm not letting go   Ella –
    I'm not letting go –

JONAH. ELLA, GET THE FUCK OFF ME!

(**JONAH** *shoves his daughter.*)

Ella, I –

(**ELLA** *exits.* **GERALDINE** *follows.*)

That wasn't...

(**RUBEN** *disappears.* **JONAH** *turns to* **SAM.***)

I don't know what that...

(Mount Morris Park materializes.)

(A bench.)

(A long moment.)

SAM. My brother, Kurt, got married in June.

I don't know if I told you I have a brother.

*(**JONAH** shakes his head no.)*

Yeah, well, I do. Anyway, he asked me to be the best man at his wedding, which I was surprised by because, well, because we're this close.

*(**SAM** gestures, fingers wide apart.)*

And screw tradition, right? Have whoever you want as yr best man.

I mean, I would've been happy to be an usher or a nothing even, but, no... best man. And as you probably know one of the presumed duties of the best man is to organize the bachelor party, which in my brother's case meant dancers. Lots of dancers. And lots of beer. My two favorite things. But that's what he wanted so that's what I planned.

I booked a private room at a club near Columbus and I sat there with him and his friends while they got incredibly drunk and incredibly stupid and it was... I mean, I don't have the words for what it was. And after maybe three hours, my brother, in his drunken generosity, calls this girl, excuse me, woman, he calls this woman over, and he says to her, "my baby brother's never had a lap dance before." And I saw where this was going and I was like, "no, no thanks, it's really okay." And I tried to leave. I stood up to go. I said, "I'll wait in the car," but they grabbed me. Kurt and his friends grabbed me and held me down. They pinned me to the booth. They literally pinned me down... One of his friends poured his beer...

(Slight beat.)

SAM. And in that filthy place, with a topless dancer between my legs, I decided never to go home again.

(Beat.)

My parents don't know. I never told them about that night or my decision. They call once a week. My mom asks if I'm eating. My dad asks about the weather. But they never ask when I'm coming home.

(Beat.)

And it's this place yr supposed to be able to go, you know? Home. This warm place, like yr grandmother was describing at dinner. But I don't feel that. Home is not an easy place for me.

(Slight beat.)

So I guess all of that's to say that I think I kind of understand… That I get maybe why you feel…

(Beat.)

But maybe not.

*(A long moment and then **JONAH** takes **SAM**'s hand.)*

*(**GERALDINE**'s brownstone materializes.)*

ELLA. Nana?

GERALDINE. Yes, baby?

ELLA. How long do people stay sad?

GERALDINE. What do you mean?

ELLA. I mean, like how long does it last?

GERALDINE. Well, I suppose it depends on the person and on what the person is sad about.

ELLA. Will Daddy be sad for a very long time?

GERALDINE. I think... I think that yr father is very lucky to have someone in his life who loves him enough to ask that question.

(*Beat.*)

You know he loves you, right? Even when he's sad. Even when he yells.

ELLA. Yeah, I know. I shouldn't have grabbed his leg though.

GERALDINE. Probably not. But I don't think any of us were at our best this evening.

ELLA. We'll do better next time.

GERALDINE. (*With a slight smile.*) Yes, we'll do better next time.

JONAH. We were fighting about my mom, which is pretty standard for us. "All roads lead to Shay."

(**JONAH** *looks at* **SAM.**)

That was her name. Shay.

SAM. Pretty.

JONAH. Yeah.

(*Slight beat.*)

Her and my dad were living with my grandma to save money after I was born. But living with Geraldine comes with rules. A lot of rules. And I guess at some point they got tired of following them, so they left.

SAM. Where'd they go?

JONAH. Who knows. Far, far away, never to be seen or heard from again.

ELLA. Nana?

GERALDINE. Uh huh?

ELLA. Do you think Daddy and Mr. Sam are boyfriends?

GERALDINE. Little girl, what do you know about boyfriends?

ELLA. Everybody knows about boyfriends, Nana. Almost all the girls in my class have one.

GERALDINE. Is that right?

ELLA. Uh huh. My friend Katie has two.

GERALDINE. Well, all right for Katie.

> *(Slight beat.)*

Do *you* have a boyfriend?

ELLA. No. Some boys like me, but...

GERALDINE. But what?

ELLA. I don't know. Most of them just act so stupid all the time.

> *(**GERALDINE** laughs.)*

What? They do! What's so funny?

GERALDINE. Nothing, baby.

ELLA. But yr laughing.

GERALDINE. I just wish I'd been as smart as you when I was yr age.

JONAH. And then I'm in high school and me and my best friend, Q, decide to... you know. 'Cause it's our junior year and neither of us wants to go off to college without having had sex.

SAM. Understandable.

JONAH. Yeah, only we were stupid. Like really really stupid. And Q got pregnant. And she had the baby even though her parents were like "no way." And then after graduation she took off for California. It turns out she wasn't ready to be a mom.

(Slight beat.)

Anyway, Geraldine adopted Ella the same way she adopted me after my mom left – once again, making up for the mistakes of others. And it's like she screwed up with her kid, right? With my mom. So she put all this energy into me. And then I screwed up with Ella –

SAM. You didn't screw up.

JONAH. Yeah, tell that to Geraldine.

SAM. Look, Ella's a great kid. And that greatness comes from somewhere.

*(He points at **JONAH**.)*

You should be proud. Yr making it work. Yr maintaining a family.

JONAH. Maintaining's a stretch.

SAM. You know what I mean.

(Slight beat.)

I can barely sustain a goldfish, let alone a kid. Or a relationship, for that matter.

JONAH. Yeah, well, they're not exactly my strong point either.

ELLA. Daddy used to be boyfriends with Ruben before, didn't he?

GERALDINE. Yes, he did.

ELLA. But not anymore.

GERALDINE. No, not anymore.

ELLA. Why not? Did they stop liking each other or something?

GERALDINE. Or something.

ELLA. Like what?

GERALDINE. So many questions tonight.

ELLA. You said it was good to ask questions.

GERALDINE. Yr right, I did.

ELLA. So?

(**ELLA** *turns to face* **GERALDINE.**)

Nana, so?

GERALDINE. Sometimes relationships change. Most of the time it happens naturally. Over time. It's like the way you don't have playdates with a lot of yr pre-school friends anymore. You didn't stop liking them, did you?

ELLA. No.

GERALDINE. Right, you just don't see them as much anymore because you've all grown up and gone on to different schools, made new friends.

ELLA. But what about Daddy?

GERALDINE. What happened to yr father is not appropriate for eight-year-old ears.

ELLA. But I'm almost nine!

GERALDINE. That's still too young.

ELLA. But why? Why can't I be older now?

GERALDINE. Trust me, it'll happen. Now turn yr head forward so I can finish this hair.

(*Beat.*)

ELLA. I think it's because Ruben was stupid.

GERALDINE. What?

ELLA. Like the boys at my school. I think that's the reason they're not boyfriends anymore because Ruben did something really stupid.

>*(**ELLA** turns her head.)*

Am I right?

>*(**GERALDINE** gives **ELLA** a look. **ELLA** turns back around.)*

I bet I'm right.

>*(Beat.)*

If Daddy decides he doesn't want Mr. Sam to be his boyfriend, I think I'll let him be mine.

>*(**GERALDINE** laughs.)*

What? Nana, what?

GERALDINE. Little girl, you are something else!

>*(Later that night.)*

>*(**JONAH** enters his apartment.)*

>*(He locks the door – all three locks.)*

>*(He takes a breath.)*

>*(He smiles to himself.)*

>*(**GERALDINE** flips open her phone and dials a number.)*

>*(**JONAH** checks, then answers.)*

JONAH. Hi.

GERALDINE. *(Shock.)* You picked up.

JONAH. I did.

>*(Slight beat.)*

JONAH. Nana –?

GERALDINE. Yes, sorry, I'm just... I'm just so used to getting yr voicemail.

JONAH. Yeah, well, you got me this time.

GERALDINE. Right. I got you.

(A moment.)

GERALDINE. Jonah, I wanted   **JONAH.** Did you need
to say –   something or –?
Oh. Sorry –

JONAH. Nah, ladies first.

GERALDINE. I just wanted to say... that what happened tonight... that's not what I wanted to have happen.

JONAH. Yeah, me either.

(Beat.)

Is Ella okay?

GERALDINE. She's fine. She's... very forgiving.

GERALDINE & JONAH. Thank God.

(Beat.)

GERALDINE. You get home okay?

JONAH. Yeah, just walked in.

GERALDINE. Is Sam with you?

JONAH. Nana!

GERALDINE. What? I'm just asking. You can't blame me for asking.

JONAH. Yes, I can. I totally can.

(A shared smile and then –)

GERALDINE. You know, you can talk to me, right? About whatever. I know I can be a wall –

JONAH. Sure can –

GERALDINE. But little boy, so can you. We're alike in that way.

(*Beat.*)

We used to talk more remember? Back before things got...

I miss that.

JONAH. Nana –

GERALDINE. And I know I'm being mooshy and you hate / mooshy –

JONAH. I don't hate mooshy.

(**RUBEN** *appears. He dials a number.*)

GERALDINE. It's just that all this distance...

(*A ring tone.* **JONAH** *is receiving another call. He checks the number.*)

It just seems so / unnecessary –

JONAH. Nana, I have to go.

GERALDINE. Jonah, we're in the middle of a conversation –

JONAH. I know, I'm sorry, but I –

GERALDINE. I'm trying to talk to you –

JONAH. Yeah, I know, but –

GERALDINE. But what, Jonah? / But what –?

JONAH. I'll call you back.

(*Beat.*)

GERALDINE. Fine. Call me back.

*(**GERALDINE** closes her phone. **JONAH** is automatically connected to the second call.)*

RUBEN. Hey. I wasn't sure you were gonna answer.

(Slight beat.)

Jonah –?

JONAH. Look,

I only picked up to tell you we're not doing this anymore.

You calling.

Me picking up.

No more.

Not again.

Ever.

You hear me?

Never again.

*(**JONAH** wavers.)*

Ruben?

Ruben, did you hear what I said –?

RUBEN. Let me over.

JONAH. Let you over? Are you crazy? Fuck, no. And fuck you.

RUBEN. Give me a reason.

JONAH. What do you mean give you / a reason –?

RUBEN. Give me a reason why I shouldn't come over. And not a reason from yr lawyer or yr grandma. A reason from you. You do that... and I'm gone. Poof. Out of yr life.

(Beat.)

Jonah?

> *(Beat.)*

Look, what happened before was...

That wasn't me. You know that wasn't me.

I'd never hurt you.

Never.

You know that.

I love you, J.

I've been loving you.

> *(Beat.)*

Let me over.

> *(We hear a lock turn.)*

Let me over.

> *(We hear a lock turn.)*

Let me over.

> *(We hear a lock turn.)*

> (**JONAH** *and* **RUBEN** *lower their phones and look at each other for the first time.*)

RUBEN. Hey.

JONAH. Hi.

> (**RUBEN** *takes a step toward* **JONAH**, **JONAH** *moves away.*)

RUBEN. Nice digs.

Geraldine?

JONAH. Uh... yeah.

RUBEN. Figures.

>   (**RUBEN** *notices the chain around* **JONAH**'s
>   *neck.*)

Huh.

JONAH. What?

RUBEN. Yr still wearing it.

JONAH. Wearing what?

RUBEN. The chain, boy. The chain.

>   (**JONAH** *touches the chain around his neck.*)

JONAH. Oh. Yeah.

RUBEN. It still looks good.

>   (*A moment and then* **RUBEN** *moves toward*
>   **JONAH.**)

JONAH. Ruben, don't.

>   (**RUBEN** *recalibrates.*)

RUBEN. How about this? I'll be gentle, that sound good?
'Cause I can be gentle, I can, like a lamb. I swear.

JONAH. Ruben, I...

RUBEN. See.

>   (**RUBEN** *kisses* **JONAH**'s *cheek.*)

See how gentle I can be?

>   (**RUBEN** *kisses* **JONAH**'s *other cheek, then his
>   eyelids, then his mouth.*)

>   (*Eventually,* **JONAH** *gives in to* **RUBEN**'s *kisses.*)

>   (**RUBEN** *pushes* **JONAH** *back on the bed, then
>   begins to kiss his way down* **JONAH**'s *body.*)

*(**RUBEN** removes his belt.)*

(Their engagement intensifies.)

JONAH. Ruben...

(Beat.)

Ruben, please, I...

(Beat.)

Ruben, wait –

RUBEN. Nah, J. I'm through waiting.

*(**RUBEN** unzips his pants and pulls at **JONAH**'s underwear. **JONAH** resists.)*

JONAH. Ruben, stop –

RUBEN. Jonah, what the / fuck –!

JONAH. I said, fucking STOP!

*(**JONAH** pushes **RUBEN** off.)*

*(A moment and then he sees a change on **RUBEN**'s face, a change he's seen before.)*

I'm sorry, I –

RUBEN. Are you fucking serious?

JONAH. Ruben, I just –

RUBEN. You just what? Changed yr mind?

(Sudden, violent.)

Fuck, J, you always do this to me –

JONAH. Always / do what –?

RUBEN. You get me all wound up and then...

I came all the way from Euclid.

RUBEN. An hour and a half on the train just to see you –

JONAH. I'm sorry –

RUBEN. Yr a cock teasing little bitch, you know that?

Hot one minute, cold the next.

You think I can't do better?

Is that what you think?

That I can't do better than yr ass?

Shit, motherfucker.

I have.

> (**JONAH** *is visibly shaken.*)

I love you, J.

I do.

But yr a fucking mental case.

> (**RUBEN** *exits the apartment, slamming the door.* **JONAH** *moves to the door and locks it – all three locks.*)

JONAH. Fuck.

> *(Beat.)*

Fuck.

> (**JONAH** *breaks.*)
>
> *(A beep.)*

GERALDINE. *(Pre-recorded voicemail.)* "Jonah, baby,

It's Nana.

I'm just calling to confirm that you are picking up Ella from school this afternoon.

She's out at two thirty.

Two thirty.

T-W-O thirty.

I know we discussed it.

I know.

And I know that yr on it.

I know.

But you know me.

I'm a double-checker from way back.

Please bring her a snack.

Nothing too filling.

I don't want to ruin her dinner.

Something good to fill her body with.

Not hotdogs.

Call me if you have questions.

Love, Grandma."

> (**JONAH** *and* **ELLA** *appear.* **JONAH** *has his cane.*)

ELLA. Do you even know how to do afterschool pick-up?

JONAH. I imagine it's a lot like picking you up from dance class.

ELLA. No, Daddy, it's totally different.

JONAH. Totally different? How is it totally / different –?

ELLA. Well, first you have to bring an afterschool snack for afterschool pick up –

> (**ELLA***'s words have an immediate effect on* **JONAH.***)*

JONAH. *(Under his breath.)* Aw, shit.

ELLA. You know, like apple slices or raisins –

JONAH. *(Under his breath.)* Shit, shit, shit –

ELLA. My favorite snack is popcorn. Did you bring popcorn for snack, Daddy?

JONAH. Um, well no, not exactly.

ELLA. Did you bring anything?

JONAH. Of course. Let me just…

> (**JONAH** *searches his pockets. He produces a box of Tic Tacs.**)

You like Tic Tacs, right?

ELLA. For snack?

JONAH. Why not? It's like eating dessert first.

> (**JONAH** *shakes a few mints into* **ELLA**'*s palm.*)

ELLA. I only like the orange ones.

JONAH. Beggars can't be choosers.

> *(They eat.)*

ELLA. This is a very disappointing afterschool snack.

JONAH. Hey, don't talk with yr mouth full.

> *(A moment and then –)*

So yr good then?

ELLA. Yeah, I'm good, Nana's good, everybody's good.

JONAH. Good.

ELLA. Are you?

---

* A license to produce *the bandaged place* does not include a license to publicly display any branded logos or trademarked images. Licensees must acquire rights for any logos and/or images or create their own.

JONAH. Yeah, of course.

> (**ELLA** *gives her father a look.*)

What? Do I not look good? Is it my hair?

ELLA. Yr using yr cane again.

JONAH. I use my cane every day, Belly.

ELLA. You didn't use it after dance class the last time. The time you came to dinner? Remember? You didn't use it then. I thought yr knee was getting better.

JONAH. It is.

ELLA. Then why do you need it?

> (**JONAH** *doesn't have a response. They continue to eat Tic Tacs. Eventually –*)

JONAH. Hey, Ella?

ELLA. Yes, Daddy?

JONAH. I wanted to talk to you.

ELLA. About what?

JONAH. Well, about...

> (*Slight beat.*)

Ella, you know that I would never...

ELLA. Never what?

JONAH. I just want to say. Need to say. That I would never hurt you. Ever. And that despite my hiccups as a father, I never want to do wrong by you. And I won't to the best of my ability. I promise.

> (*Slight beat.*)

Do you understand?

ELLA. You have the hiccups?

JONAH. What?

ELLA. You said you have the hiccups.

JONAH. Oh, no, Ella, I was talking / about –

ELLA. 'Cause Miss Kennedy says the best thing for hiccups is to hold yr breath and plug yr ears and drink water all at the same time.

> (**JONAH** *looks at* **ELLA**.)

Daddy? Did you hear me? About the hiccups?

> (**JONAH** *hugs his daughter as his apartment materializes.*)
>
> (*Later that night.*)
>
> (**JONAH** *and* **SAM** *have been eating take-out and drinking whiskey.*)

JONAH. And then she said, "Miss Kennedy says that's the best way to get rid of the hiccups."

SAM. She didn't.

JONAH. She did. I delivered this whole speech. That I'd practiced, mind you –

SAM. Of course –

JONAH. And all she heard was that her daddy had the hiccups.

SAM. That's hilarious. Incredibly cute and hilarious.

JONAH. It was definitely something.

SAM. You know, even though she didn't fully understand yr apology –

JONAH. Like at all –

SAM. Right. Like at all. The important thing is that you *did* apologize. I mean, how many parents do that? How many people do that?

JONAH. Not enough.

SAM. Exactly. The world would be a better place if we all just apologized more.

JONAH. I'll drink to that.

(*They clink glasses and drink.*)

SAM. Hey, do you ever...?

JONAH. Do I ever what?

SAM. Uh... no, sorry, nothing. Nevermind.

JONAH. Sam.

SAM. No, really, it's stupid, it's really stupid.

JONAH. I like stupid.

(**SAM** *gives* **JONAH** *a look.*)

I do! Come on, tell me what you were gonna say.

Sam!

SAM. Fine, okay, I will, but you can't judge.

JONAH. I won't.

(**SAM** *gives* **JONAH** *a look.*)

I won't! Pinkie swear.

(**JONAH** *offers his finger.* **SAM** *chuckles...*)

SAM. Yeah, okay, pinkie swear.

(*...then reciprocates.*)

JONAH. So...?

SAM. So... I was going to ask if you ever think about where words go?

JONAH. Where words go...?

SAM. Yeah, like... okay take yr apology, for example.

JONAH. Okay...

SAM. I imagine it floating out there somewhere, reverberating in the cosmos. And I bet in like ten years it'll make its way back to Harlem and Ella will hear it for the second time and it'll mean something.

(*Slight beat.*)

See? Stupid.

JONAH. Actually. That's not stupid at all. I hope yr right.

(*Beat.*)

SAM. I had a teacher once who told me that if you don't tell the universe what you want, then it'll never come to you. And at first, I was... skeptical. I mean, the universe? Really? But the more I thought about it, the more life I lived, the more life happened to me, I figured, why not give it a shot?

JONAH. What'd you do? Run up a hill and yell at the sky *Sound of Music* style?

SAM. No. Well, I guess you could do it that way, but no. Mine was more like, write down three things you'd like to see happen then burn the list with a candle. Simple shit like that. You know, a little ceremony.

JONAH. I like a ceremony.

SAM. Who doesn't like a ceremony?

(*A moment.*)

JONAH. Can I ask about yr list?

SAM. Oh, uh, yeah, sure.

(*And then, a performance –*)

My three things, in no particular order, are: One, to get my ass in gear and start auditioning again. 'Cause, frankly I've gotten comfortable with teaching. And don't get me wrong, I love it, the kids, I love them, but my body is like, "Push me! Challenge me!" And that impulse, that voice won't scream at me for forever. I mean, eventually my body'll be like, "Sit the fuck down!"

JONAH. I hear that.

(*Beat.*)

Two?

SAM. Two! Get out more. See things. Do people.

JONAH. You don't already? I mean, you seem –

SAM. Socially inclined? Yeah, it's an act. A glorious act. In all honesty, I just always want to be home. But not like my living room home – 'cause that's a whole other thing, my apartment situation – I mean like in my room. In my bed. Because cable beats out the Met any day of the week.

JONAH. I hear you.

SAM. Okay!

JONAH. And the third?

SAM. (*Coy.*) That one I'll never tell.

(*Beat.*)

What about you? What would be on yrs?

JONAH. Nuh-uh.

SAM. Oh, come on, I told.

JONAH. Nope.

SAM. I promise I won't judge.

(*Slight beat.*)

Pinkie swear.

(*A moment and then,* **JONAH** *concedes.*)

JONAH. Fine, but only because I need you to stop making that face.

SAM. What? This one?

> *(He makes a face, shared laughter.)*

JONAH. Okay so I think my first would be that Ella would grow up healthy and safe and unscarred by me and her grandmother and our best efforts at raising her. My second would be that that I'd be dancing, with Ephemeral or whoever. And my third... that my knee would... that I wouldn't be scared of my knee anymore.

SAM. That's a good list.

> *(A moment. Something shifts. Both men feel it.)*

> *(**SAM** changes the subject.)*

Do you have music?

JONAH. Do I...?

SAM. You know what? Nevermind. *I* do.

> *(He pulls out an iPod.)*

JONAH. What are you doing?

SAM. *We* are going to dance.

> *(**SAM** attaches it to **JONAH**'s deck. Music begins to play and **SAM** begins to move.*)*

JONAH. Oh. No. I don't think / so –

SAM. That's the whole point. To *not* think.

The point is to move.

Now come on.

---

* A license to produce *the bandaged place* does not include a performance license for any third-party or copyrighted music. Licensees should create an original composition or use music in the public domain. For further information, please see the Music and Third-Party Materials Use Note on page iii.

JONAH. Sam –

SAM. Boy, I said come on!

>   (**SAM** *moves with a kind of abandon, a freedom.* **JONAH** *is hesitant at first, but after a while, loosens. They dance together.*)

JONAH. God, I've missed this!

>   This feeling.

>   It's like…

>   Fuck, I don't even know.

SAM. It's like flying.

JONAH. What?

SAM. That's how it's always felt to me anyway.

>   Dancing?

>   Like the closest thing we have to lift off.

JONAH. Lift off.

>   I love that.

SAM. Feel free to borrow it.

JONAH. I just might.

>   (**SAM** *and* **JONAH** *are close. A moment and then* **SAM** *breaks away.*)

SAM. This was a good idea. Take-out. I love ordering in.

JONAH. Me too. And room service.

SAM. In hotels? Yes, room service is awesome.

JONAH. I should add that to my list. More room service!

SAM. More room service!

>   (**JONAH** *yawns.*)

SAM. Shit, it's late. I should go.

> (**SAM** *turns off the music.*)

Let you sleep –

JONAH. No, it was just a yawn. I'm just not breathing deeply enough. Stay.

SAM. Are you sure? 'Cause it's not a / big deal –

JONAH. Sam. Pull up a pillow.

> (**JONAH** *tosses* **SAM** *a pillow.* **SAM** *moves to the bed.*)

SAM. I really like yr apartment. I would kill to live alone.

JONAH. It's not so great.

SAM. Yr kidding, right? I think I mentioned my living situation? So I have roommates, two, and they have girlfriends, so four, and they like never leave! Like ever! Like I can't tell you how many times I've been walked in on in the bathroom. Like I'm literally on the toilet doing my thing and the bathroom door doesn't lock, right? And the landlord's like, "deal," 'cause she's a dick. So people just –

> (**SAM** *gestures.*)

And it's crazy really. 'Cause I mean you'd think people would figure it out. Like that they'd start knocking or something so as to prevent the whole peep show aspect of sharing a living space thing, but no. None of them do. And so, I mean, essentially, I live in a zoo.

> (**SAM** *looks at* **JONAH.**)

Jonah?

> (*Slight beat.*)

Jonah, are you...?

> (**JONAH** *is asleep.*)

Sweet dreams.

> (**SAM** *covers* **JONAH** *with a blanket, turns out the lights, then exits. Jonah's apartment falls away.*)

JONAH'S CELL PHONE. *(Pre-recorded.)* "The person at the number you have dialed is not available.

Please leave a message after the tone."

> *(A beep.)*

> (**RUBEN** *appears.*)

> *(He leaves a message.)*

RUBEN. Hey,

It's me.

> *(Slight beat.)*

Look,

I'm probably the last person you want to talk to after what went down the other night.

You probably won't even listen to this message, but I wanted to say that... I'm sorry.

I'm sorry I got mad

And ran my mouth

And said things that weren't true.

'Cause they weren't. They were just...

It's just that I think about you and me, about us not being together, and it just... rips me apart.

Like when you were working uptown

And just the idea of other guys having access to you, you know?

RUBEN. Guys smarter than me

With money

And connections.

And like you not seeing that these dudes were trying to fuck with you

'Cause they were definitely trying to fuck with you

And you couldn't fucking see it.

You couldn't fucking see it 'cause you could never see how beautiful you were.

How fucking beautiful

And sexy

And...

But I did.

I do.

And I know I fucked up.

I know I did,

But I can do better.

I can *be* better.

I know I can.

> *(Beat.)*

I was thinking about when we met.

Like back when we were cool and things were easy?

You remember that?

I was sitting on that stoop in the West Village

And I saw you coming down the block looking sexy as fuck,

Only I could tell you didn't know it.

And you passed and I watched you pass, praying,

"Dear God, make him stop."

And you did.

You sorta half turned around

And by the time you'd made it one eighty

I was there.

And I asked you if you were thirsty.

And you remember what you said?

You said, "I could drink."

(Slight beat.)

That night was the beginning of something I'd never had before.

Something I'd never felt before that night

And that stoop

And that street before you.

I saw you and I thought, "there he is."

And you know I don't talk this way.

It's the furthest thing from me.

But I felt it.

And you felt it.

I know you did.

'Cause we fit, Jonah.

From jump we fit.

And regardless of whatever's gone down between us.

Whatever the bullshit...

That fit doesn't go away.

(Monday.)

(After dance class.)

*(***RUBEN*** waits.)*

*(After a while, ***ELLA*** appears.)*

RUBEN. Belly!

ELLA. Ruben?

RUBEN. Hey, babygirl!

ELLA. What are you doing here?

RUBEN. What do you think? I came to see you.

ELLA. You did?

RUBEN. I did. And you know what else?

ELLA. What?

RUBEN. I brought you a present.

*(***RUBEN*** reveals a small bag.)*

ELLA. Popcorn! My favorite snack. You remembered.

RUBEN. Of course, I remembered.

ELLA. Thank you.

RUBEN. Yr welcome. Hey, let me get a good look at you.

*(***ELLA*** twirls.)*

You know what?

ELLA. What?

RUBEN. I think you grew a whole inch since the last time
I saw you.

ELLA. Nuh-uh!

RUBEN. Yep, a whole inch. Yr almost as tall as me.

ELLA. No!

RUBEN. For serious!

ELLA. Yr so silly, Ruben.

RUBEN. That's me. Silly, Ruben.

> *(Beat.)*

So I guess yr daddy's been real busy?

ELLA. I guess...

RUBEN. He lost his phone –?

ELLA. Mr. Sam!

> *(**SAM** appears.)*

Ruben, this is my teacher, Mr. Sam. Mr. Sam, this is Ruben.

SAM. Hi.

RUBEN. Hey.

SAM. You know Ella from...?

ELLA. Ruben knows my daddy.

RUBEN. That's right, me and Ella's father go way back. I was just in the neighborhood and I remembered that Ella had class over here so I thought I'd stop by and say hello. We haven't seen each other in a minute.

SAM. I see.

RUBEN. *(To **ELLA**.)* I was hoping to maybe see yr daddy, too. Is he picking you up today –?

> *(**GERALDINE** appears.)*

SAM. Geraldine.

> *(**RUBEN** turns. **GERALDINE** sees him and freezes.)*

RUBEN. Hey there, Miss Irby, what's / good –?

GERALDINE. Sam, take Ella inside.

SAM. What –?   **RUBEN.** Are you serious right now –?

GERALDINE. Get her out of here now!

ELLA. Nana?

SAM. Come on, Ella.

> (**SAM** *exits with* **ELLA**.)

RUBEN. Look, Miss Irby, I can explain –

GERALDINE. One step closer and I'll call the police.

> (**GERALDINE** *flips open her phone.*)

I will.

> (**RUBEN** *stops.*)

My grandson might not have the wherewithal to do it, but you better believe I have the NYPD on speed dial and I will press every charge there is to press.

RUBEN. Yeah, all right, calm down. I just wanted to see my girl.

GERALDINE. You listen to me. Ella is not, never has been and never will be yr girl.

RUBEN. *(Whatever.)* Yeah, okay –

GERALDINE. No, not, yeah okay. You might've taken her to the park once or twice. You might've greased her hair. She might even light up when she sees you, but that don't mean shit.

RUBEN. Oh, no?

GERALDINE. You stay the fuck away, you hear? Stay the fuck away.

RUBEN. *(A bit of a taunt.)* Yeah, I'll take that under advisement.

*(**RUBEN** moves to exit.)*

Fucking bitch.

*(**GERALDINE** makes a decision.)*

GERALDINE. You nearly killed him.

*(This has an immediate effect on **RUBEN**. He doesn't turn back, but he stops.)*

You understand that, right? You nearly...

*(**GERALDINE** holds herself together.)*

You sat up there in the courtroom talking 'bout you love him –?

*(**RUBEN** turns.)*

RUBEN. Yeah, so –?

GERALDINE. So let him go!

(Slight beat.)

If it's true, then let my grandson go.

(A stand-off and then –)

RUBEN. Whatever.

*(**RUBEN** exits.)*

*(**GERALDINE** breaks.)*

(She gasps for air.)

(She dials a number.)

JONAH'S CELL PHONE. *(Pre-recorded.)* "The person at the number you have dialed is not available –"

*(**GERALDINE** snaps her phone shut.)*

GERALDINE. Damn-it, Jonah! Pick up yr fucking phone!

(A moment and then she dials again.)

JONAH'S CELL PHONE. *(Pre-recorded.)* "The person at the number you have dialed is not available.

Please leave a message after the tone."

(A beep.)

*(**GERALDINE** leaves a message.)*

GERALDINE. Jonah, I...

*(**GERALDINE** makes a decision.)*

Call me back when you get this, okay? We need to talk.

*(**GERALDINE** closes her phone and exits.)*

(Later.)

(Jonah's apartment materializes.)

*(**SAM** appears.)*

JONAH. It's just he started to get mad about little things.

Like Ephemeral was rehearsing up in Harlem

And me and him were living all the way out in Brooklyn

At the Euclid stop on the C –

SAM. East New York.

JONAH. Yeah, East New York.

And he'd get so mad when I wouldn't get home until eleven thirty sometimes if we were rehearsing late.

And he'd yell

And he'd push me around

And accuse me of cheating on him with other dancers in the company.

(Slight beat.)

And then he burned my wallet.

(**SAM** *gives* **JONAH** *a look.*)

Yeah, like with my cash

And my debit card

And my Metro card

So I couldn't get away.

And then he got drunk one night...

And he stabbed me with a kitchen knife.

SAM. He... sorry, he what –?

JONAH. Six times.

(**SAM** *gives* **JONAH** *a look.*)

Yeah. Six.

And I think...

I think mostly, I was embarrassed, you know?

Because I'd made this big show of moving out

Of moving away from Geraldine

And moving in with this man who turned out to be...

Well, clearly not who I thought he was.

(*Geraldine's apartment materializes.*)

ELLA. Nana?

GERALDINE. Yes, baby?

ELLA. Is Ruben bad?

GERALDINE. What?

ELLA. Is Ruben bad?

'Cause yr voice sounded funny after class.

ELLA. Like you were scared.

Like you were scared of Ruben.

Only Ruben's not scary.

I don't think he's scary.

> *(Slight beat.)*

Is he scary?

JONAH. And when I say it out loud now it's like, of course, you know?

Like, of course that happened.

I fucking walked right into it.

How the fuck didn't I see it coming?

How the fuck?

But I didn't.

ELLA. Did Ruben hurt Daddy?

(Forceful.) Nana, did you hear me about Ruben –?

GERALDINE. Yes, baby. I heard you.

> *(**GERALDINE** makes a decision.)*

And yes, he did. Ruben hurt yr daddy very badly.

JONAH. And the fact is that even after everything

The hospital

And the physical therapy

And the therapy therapy

And the humiliation

After all of that

I still want him.

> *(**JONAH** recalibrates.)*

Nah, my body still wants him.

> *(Beat.)*

And how fucked up is that, right?

I mean, how fucked up is –

> (**SAM** *kisses* **JONAH**.)

SAM. I'm sorry, I just...

Um...

I don't know why I...

> (**JONAH** *kisses* **SAM**.)
>
> *(And then –)*
>
> (**SAM** *kisses* **JONAH** *back*.)
>
> *(It's sweet at first and then it morphs into something else entirely.)*
>
> *(Something passionate, yes, but also, and more importantly, something safe and real and meant.)*
>
> *(Clothes are removed.)*
>
> *(The men tumble into bed.)*

GERALDINE. Dear heavenly Father,

We've been here before

You and I

Deep in the valley of the shadow of death

And I know You said that I don't have to fear

That You promised Yr rod and staff would comfort me

But

Lord

GERALDINE. I don't feel it

That comfort.

No matter how hard I try.

What I feel is fear.

Fear for my grandson

Fear for...

And I know,

I know, that faith isn't feeling

But I can't help it

Not today

And so I'm gonna need Yr help

I'm gonna need more than a rod and a staff

I'm gonna need a miracle

A burning bush

A pillar of cloud

I'm gonna need You to turn some water into wine

'Cause

I'm not sure that anything less is gonna turn the tide

And Father God

We need a tide turn.

(Later.)

SAM. So... I've never been set up by an eight-year-old before.

JONAH. Yes, well, Ella is advanced for her age.

SAM. She is. Quite advanced.

(Beat.)

I hope this is okay. You know, given everything.

JONAH. Given everything, this is very okay.

>(**SAM** *smiles.*)

SAM. Okay.

>(**JONAH** *smiles.*)

JONAH. Okay.

>(*Beat.*)

SAM. So I'm already regretting this, but I should probably go home and shower before class.

JONAH. Sure. Professionalism demands.

SAM. That, and my level ones are observant as fuck. They'll wonder why I'm wearing the same clothes two days in a row.

>(**JONAH** *laughs.*)

I'll never hear the end of it.

JONAH. Well, in that case...

>(*Slight beat.*)

Thanks for staying.

SAM. Thanks for kissing me.

>(*They kiss again.*)

Bye.

>(**SAM** *exits.*)

>(**JONAH** *basks in the afterglow.*)

>(*Eventually, his fingers find the chain around his neck and his countenance changes.*)

>(*He produces his phone.*)

(He considers it, then flips the device open.)

(He dials a number.)

(He gets Ruben's voicemail.)

RUBEN'S VOICEMAIL. *(Pre-recorded.)* "Yo, what's good?"

(A beep.)

*(**JONAH** leaves a message.)*

JONAH. I know you saw Ella.

You thought I wouldn't find out?

That's some fucked up shit, Ruben.

Even for you, that's...

That's fucked up.

Putting a kid in the middle of us

Of what used to be us.

And I know.

I know that you were a part of her life before

But we ain't together anymore

And you made damn sure we wouldn't be ever again.

You did that so...

*(**RUBEN** appears.)*

And yeah, I loved you.

I probably still do.

And I might never stop

But not all love is good love.

Not all love makes you feel safe.

And that's the whole point so...

So if I see or hear from you again

Or if I hear that you said shit to my daughter when I wasn't around to protect her

I'm calling the cops.

You hear me?

I'm calling the cops and I'm telling them to lock yr ass up this time.

I'm saying no and I mean it this time.

> *(Music.*)*
>
> *(**JONAH** and **RUBEN** begin to move.)*
>
> *(They come together.)*
>
> *(They pull apart.)*
>
> *(It is a romance.)*
>
> *(It is a struggle.)*
>
> *(Eventually, **JONAH** dispels **RUBEN**.)*
>
> *(Finally free, he dances alone.)*
>
> *(It is virtuosic.)*
>
> *(He removes the chain from around his neck and drops it to the floor.)*
>
> *(He breathes.)*
>
> *(His phone starts to ring.)*

Shit.

Coming, coming...

---

* A license to produce *the bandaged place* does not include a performance license for any third-party or copyrighted music. Licensees should create an original composition or use music in the public domain. For further information, please see the Music and Third-Party Materials Use Note on page iii.

(**JONAH** *checks the number, then answers.*)

JONAH. Hey, are you downstairs?

(*A reply.*)

Cool.

(*A reply.*)

Yeah, almost.

(*A reply.*)

No, don't come up. You'll just distract me.

(*A reply.*)

Yeah, you will. I'm telling you, you will.

(**JONAH** *smiles.*)

Seriously, Sam. I'll be down in two minutes. Even less if you hang up the damn phone.

(*A reply.*)

Okay, bye.

(**JONAH** *pulls on clothes and shoes then moves to the door and exits. The door closes. We hear the sound of a key turning in the outside lock. And then –*)

(*Offstage.*) Shit, Ruben. What are you doing here?

RUBEN. (*Offstage.*) I got yr message. I had to listen to it twice. It didn't sound like you.

JONAH. (*Offstage.*) I told you I'd call the cops / if you showed up here –

RUBEN. (*Offstage.*) You going somewhere? With Mr. Sam? Yeah, I read that bitch minute one. He's cute, I guess. If you like that sort of thing, tutu-wearing faggots, and I know you do.

JONAH. *(Offstage.)* I'm calling / the cops –

RUBEN. *(Offstage.)* You ain't doing shit.

(The sound of physical struggle.)

(And then the sound of Jonah's cell phone shattering against a wall.)

JONAH. *(Offstage.)* Ruben, please.

RUBEN. *(Offstage.)* I fucking loved you, J.

No one will ever love you like I loved you.

(The sound of **RUBEN** *beating* **JONAH**.*)*

(The sound of fists against flesh.)

(The sound of **JONAH** *crying out.)*

(This goes on for some time.)

(And then silence.)

(Before the sound of police sirens and flashing lights overwhelm the space.)

(Later.)

(A hospital room materializes.)

*(***JONAH*** is asleep.)*

(His face is bruised.)

(His leg is in a brace.)

*(***SAM*** and* **GERALDINE** *are asleep in nearby chairs.)*

*(***JONAH*** wakes.)*

(He attempts to sit up and immediately winces in pain.)

*(***SAM*** stirs.)*

SAM. Hey.

JONAH. Hi.

SAM. They gave you the good drugs. You've been out for hours.

JONAH. They let you stay.

SAM. Geraldine threw a fit. She was like, "I don't give a shit about the rules." They made an exception.

JONAH. I'm glad.

SAM. Me too. How do you feel?

JONAH. Like I got my shit fucked up by my ex.

SAM. I'm glad you haven't lost yr sense of humor.

(**JONAH** *laughs then winces.*)

Sorry.

JONAH. It's okay. You just might have to take it easy with the jokes.

SAM. I can do that.

(*Beat.*)

I'm sorry this happened to you.

I'm sorry about yr leg –

JONAH. It's okay.

SAM. Yr a dancer, Jonah, it's not okay –

JONAH. (*Please stop.*) Sam.

(*Beat.*)

SAM. I'm sorry I didn't get to you sooner.

JONAH. There was nothing you could've done –

SAM. I should've come up.

JONAH. I told you not to.

SAM. *(Louder than intended.)* I should've come up anyway!

>(**GERALDINE** *stirs.*)

GERALDINE. Yr awake.

JONAH. Yeah.

>*(A moment and then –)*

SAM. I'm gonna go raid the vending machine. Does anyone need anything?

JONAH. I'm good.

GERALDINE. Thank you, Sam.

>(**SAM** *exits. A long moment.*)

JONAH. Nana, I...

>(**GERALDINE** *holds up a hand to silence her grandson.*)

GERALDINE. I've never told you this before

But the day yr mother left...

We fought about you.

>*(Beat.)*

It was late.

I remember it was late

And I heard you crying

And it woke me up.

>*(Slight beat.)*

Now at that time

You, yr mother and yr father

GERALDINE. Stayed up on the third floor.

It was just one big room back then.

And I remember laying in my bed for the longest time just waiting for it to stop

For you to stop

For Shay to do something to make you stop

But you didn't.

You didn't.

You just kept right on screaming

And after a while I just couldn't take it anymore.

I remember thinking, "what the hell is going on up there?"

And so I got out of bed and I climbed the stairs

And there you were in yr crib

Just a hollering

Red-faced and hollering

Fists balled.

> *(Beat.)*

And Shay and Kenny were passed out on the floor

Coked out of their minds.

And so I picked you up and I took you downstairs with me.

> *(Beat.)*

The next day Shay and Kenny came at me

Talking about I stole you from them

Talking about

Who do I think I am, taking their child

What right do I have to take their child.

And I said, "yr child? Yr child was screaming his head off and y'all were laid out."

And Shay was all like, "momma, it ain't none of yr business what we do or how we do it."

And I said to her, "yr business is my business as long as yr living in my house."

And many less savory things.

Things I'm embarrassed about.

Things I'm ashamed of.

>   *(Beat.)*

They were gone by dinner.

>   *(Beat.)*

History repeating itself...

>   *(Beat.)*

Jonah, I've made a lot of mistakes.

More than I'd like to admit.

But everything I've done I've done to...

I did for...

And I never meant to...

>   *(Beat.)*

Little boy,

You are so so precious.

>   *(**JONAH** breaks.)*

>   *(**GERALDINE** moves to her grandson.)*

>   *(She takes his hand.)*

GERALDINE. You are.

You and yr mother and yr daughter.

And I haven't told you that enough.

I didn't tell Shay that enough.

> *(Beat.)*

Hey, look at me.

Jonah, look at me.

> (**JONAH** *looks at his grandmother.*)

Do you remember the story of yr name?

The story of Jonah

The man who was swallowed up by a whale?

You remember?

> (**JONAH** *nods his head.*)

Yeah, well

That's not the end of the story

'Cause eventually Jonah cried out.

From the belly of that whale Jonah cried out to God

And the whale –

JONAH. Spit him out.

GERALDINE. Yes, he spit him out.

God gave Jonah a second chance.

Just like he's given you.

Just like he's given me.

> (**GERALDINE** *kisses* **JONAH**'s *forehead.*)
>
> (**ELLA** *appears.*)

(She has a hotdog on a tray.)

(She sits near her father.)

ELLA. Are you sure it's okay for me to eat this?

JONAH. Yes, I'm sure.

ELLA. For real?

JONAH. Yes, Ella, for real. I asked yr grandmother.

ELLA. And she said it was okay?

JONAH. She did.

ELLA. Even though she hates hotdogs and thinks they're bad?

JONAH. Even though she hates hotdogs and thinks they're bad.

ELLA. And even though they have pig lips in them?

JONAH. Even though it is *rumored* that hotdogs *may* contain pig lips, yes. I mean, if you don't want it –

> *(**JONAH** reaches for **ELLA***'s hotdog. **ELLA** *takes a huge bite.)*

That's what I thought.

> *(**JONAH** watches his daughter enjoy her food.)*

How is it?

ELLA. So good!

> *(She eats. And then –)*

Daddy?

JONAH. Yes, Ella?

ELLA. Is it true you could have died?

JONAH. What?

ELLA. When we were in the hallway outside yr room one of the nurses said that you could have died.

JONAH. I don't think you were supposed to hear that.

ELLA. But is it true?

> *(Slight beat.)*

Nana said that the doctor had to sew you up the last time you were in the hospital, the time before this time, remember?

> **(JONAH** *nods yes.)*

She said that the scars are bumpy like when you run yr hand over the globe in my room. She said that yr scars feel like mountains.

> *(Beat.)*

Would it be okay if I...?

JONAH. If you what, Belly?

ELLA. Touched them?

> *(A long moment and then* **JONAH** *exposes a scar.)*
>
> **(ELLA** *touches it.)*
>
> **(JONAH** *exposes another scar.)*
>
> **(ELLA** *touches it.)*
>
> *(Then she brings her fingers to her lips and presses them to the wound.)*

All better.

> *(A beat and then* **JONAH** *and* **ELLA** *embrace as the lights fade to black.)*

End of Play